The Tale of EVERGREEN

BY
Sariah Dangleben

ART
Jitumoni Goswami

D1710144

"Good Morning Mr. Sun" I said as I stood up from my soft bed and took in the sweet morning air. Today was a sunny spring day and the sky was cloudless. I just knew today would be perfect.

I threw on some clean clothes and headed to Olive's room. My sister was the only one who understood me. Most people say I have my head in the clouds. My own mother must have told me a million times "Opal all you do is daydream." What they don't know is that I'm not dreaming; Evergreen is real "Good morning Opal," I heard my sister say as she exited her room. "Good morning" I responded "Let's go to the Evergreen" Olive said as we both ran down the stairs. "Be back by sundown" my mother called out as we left the house. Through the door and out we went. We ran through the garden then to the woods and we soon arrived at the tree. You see, this tree is no ordinary tree; this tree is the door to a new world all you have to do is say the magic words. "Take me to the land of green and magical trees," Olive and I said in sync. In the blink of an eye the mossy wooden barked turned into a door. We opened the door and took a step inside. "What happened?" Olive said in confusion and shock. The land was once known to be full of green trees, Magic flowers and wild fairies was now black,The goblins, gremlins, fairies and trolls were nowhere to be seen .The moss village was left empty. The bakers, blacksmiths and farmers were gone. Leaving their bakeries, workshops and farms vacant. "There isn't a creature or animal in sight," I said in complete shock. Olive and I walked through the ghost town completely speechless.

We continued to walk until we heard a faint noise in

the distance. "What do I do?, what do I do?" the disembodied voice repeated in a frantic tone. Olive and I walked to the source of the noise. "Fletcher?" I called out. "Oh thank God you're here," the small warlock said. "What happened to Evergreen?" Olive questioned "Evil" he said as he stepped towards us "Pure evil, someone used black magic to curse the forest. I've used all the spells I know and none has stopped this plague from spreading". "Why would someone do this?" Olive said, with pain in her voice. "All the villagers have lost their energy due to this curse so it must be an outside force. It didn't affect me, of course, I used a protection spell but it was far too weak to save us all" Fletcher said as he touched the black goo dripping from the tree". "Who else knows about

Evergreen?" I questioned.

"No one besides you two we haven't
seen anyone else here for the century"
Fletcher said as we began to walk through
the forest. "How do we fix this?" Olive
said "we have to find lotus pond," Fletcher
answered. "Well what are you waiting for?
Let's go save evergreen." "Well, we have
one problem," Fletcher mentioned.
"We don't know where the lotus is."
"Seriously, I thought you knew where
it was!" Olive said slightly annoyed. "If
I did, I would have saved Evergreen

by now," Fletcher said as we walked through the forest. "The mushroom village has a library. The map must be there," I said.

Off to the village we went. Pass the fairy tree over the hills and around the river bend. As we arrived we noticed the curse hasn't spread to the mushroom village yet. "Perfect the curse hasn't spread here; quickly Let's get to the library before the curse beats us." We walked to the library to find the place empty. "Mr. and Ms.Enoki must

have sought out shelter from the curse" I wondered out loud. "I'm sure they wouldn't mind us coming in," Olive added. "We don't have time for chit chat, let's go," Fletcher stated as he walked over to the library ladder. "Now where is that map?"Fletcher said as he climbed up to the M section. Before I could answer we heard a frightened shy voice say "you should leave before it gets here." "Ms Enoki?" Olive called out "yes it's me," she answered. "Before we leave can you tell us where the lotus map is?" I asked. "The lotus map is being held by Quercus but he's surrounded by deer," Mr. Enoki said, as he hopped out of his hiding place. "Be careful though all the animals in evergreen have gone rogue," Ms Enoki added. "Rouge?" I questioned. "Yes the curse has caused the animals to become hostile and dangerous so be very careful when lurking in the forest" Ms Enoki answered as she pulled Mr .Enoki back into their hiding place. "We'll be fine, I can use my magic to scare them off," Fletcher boasted, as he took our hands and dragged us out of the library.

And so we went to Quercus, the talking tree. Over the Troll Bridge and past the weeping willows until finally we made it. We hid behind a bush. We were weary of the hostile deer. "Do you see the map?" Olive whispered. "I can't see it, can you fletcher?" I whispered back to Olive. "THERE IT IS!" Fletcher yelled and pointed there was the map being held by Quercus's branch though he seemed to be asleep. I held my hand over Fletcher's mouth but it was

too late the deer had been alerted of our presence and were now charging towards us. "Seriously?!" I said in an angry tone as we began to run. "Quick Fletcher, use your magic to save us," Olive said as we turned a corner. "Right, I'm on it," Fletcher said as he turned around and pulled out his wand. "Levi levi!" Fletcher casted his spell and the deer began to float. "It worked!" I said triumphantly as we headed back to Quercus. "Do you think he's asleep?" I said wondering if the curse has gotten to him as well. "I'm not sure but there's no way we can get the map if he's clinging onto it like that." Said olive "hey Quercus can we have that map?" Fletcher said as he knocked on the sleeping tree. Quercus opened his eyes slowly. "What do you need?" he said tiredly. "We wanted to know if you could hand us that map," Olive answered as she pointed towards the map. Quercus moved the branch that held the map away seemingly annoyed. "What do you need my map for?" "What do you need the map for if you don't even have legs?" Fletcher said scornfully. "I will grow legs and when I do I'll go to the mountains using this map" "Quercus if we don't get that map then we can't get to lotus pond and save the forest," Olive said with concern in her voice. "If I give you this map what can you give me in return?" Quercus questioned. "Legs I can use my magic to give you legs." Fletcher said as he took out his wand. "Really well if that's the case I'll give you the map and in return you'll give me legs." Quercus said "Deal!" I said as Fletcher began his spell. "Alakazoo!" Fletcher said and with the swish of his wand Quercus grew long wooden legs. "I have legs I can walk I can dance, I can run! Thank you here go save Evergreen" Quercus said as he handed us the map and began to dance around.

With the map in hand we set off to the mountains avoiding all dangerous animals until we hit a deadend. "I thought there was a bridge here," I said as we arrived at a creek. "I can use my magic to help us across if you would like," Fletcher offered but before he could pull out his wand Pebble and Peeper jumped out the creek. "Would you like a ride across the creek? Us frogs are fast swimmers ``Peeper offered. "Sure," I said as I hoped on Pebble's back and Olive and Fletcher

hopped on Peeper's "One thing before we get moving: do you think you can get us some magic fruit? We're running low and want to stock up before the curse spreads to our creek." Pebble said. "Sure,   I can climb that tree over there and get them for you," Olive said as she hopped off the giant frog and headed to the tree to grab the fruit. As she climbed I noticed a black aura coming our way. "Hey Olive I think you should hurry up. I think the curse is coming our way. If you don't get them soon they'll die!" I yelled up to Olive. Olive grabbed a bunch of fruit and jumped down landing on her feet. "Here you go" Olive said while smiling and handing the fruit to Peeper and hoping back on. "Let's go," I said as we headed off. As we arrived at the end of the creek we hoped off leaving the fruit with Peeper. "We'll be right here when you come back but come soon so this curse doesn't paralyze," Pebble half joked. We began to climb the mountain,but we were soon interrupted by flying gargoyles. "Duck down!" I yelled to Olive and Fletcher. Gargoyles began to swoop down from above and claw at us. "I can use a temporary invisibility spell to help us hide from the gargoyles," Fletcher said as we cowered underneath the gargoyles. "Well what are you waiting for,do it !" Olive rebutted. Fletcher waved his wand and with a few sparkles the trio turned invisible.
"Great now be very quiet," I
whispered as we

slowly began to walk up the mountain. The invisibility spell wore off as we reached the top. There we saw a crystal clear pond littered with lotus flowers and a tall cherry blossom tree hanging over the pond. "Wow," Olive said in awe. "It's so much prettier than the legend describes it to be," I said with admiration clear in my voice. "Stay where you are!" Fletcher said pointing his wand towards the two of us. "Don't move or I'll use an energy depletion

spell," Fletcher said as he walked towards the pond. "What's going on?" I asked, watching as Fletcher gathered lotuses.

"You two are as slow as snails." Fletcher said as he erupted in laughter "I was the one who cursed the forest. Did you really think an outside

force caused this," Fletcher said through laughter.

"No it can't be!" Olive said in a shaky voice. "We should have known."

I tried charging toward Fletcher but before I could reach him he used magic to

paralyze my legs.

Before I knew it my legs were numb and I fell to my knees. My legs felt flimsy and useless as I watched Fletcher walk slowly towards me. "Goodbye old friend," Fletcher said as he pointed his wand towards my head and whispered "Exzeliamous." My body began to feel weak. I heard Olive yell but my head was too hazy to understand what she said. My eyes went blurry as I laid defeated. Was this the end? What's going to happen to Evergreen? As I laid on the ground I felt my body giving up but before I could shut my eyes I heard my sister call my name . "Opal stay awake please," I heard her say as her voice broke. I started to get up but before I could Olive stopped me and handed me a piece of fruit. "What do I do with this," I said in a breathless voice.

"I kept this after climbing the tree. Eat it quickly before Fletcher comes back," Olive answered. I stared at the plump ripe fruit before sinking my teeth in. As I swallowed I felt my energy replenish and my body flourishing. I stood up on the moist grass and hugged my sister. "I thought you were dead!" Olive said with tears in her eyes. "Not so fast!" Fletcher said as he came back up from the pond. "I told the two of you not to move now you must be punished for your insubordination," Fletcher said, striking down my sister with his magic. It was then he had stepped too far. I ran towards him as adrenaline rushed through my body. "You have crossed the line!" I said firmly as I grabbed him by the collar. "Do you really want to mess with the one that has a magic wand?" Fletcher said as his feet struggled to reach the ground. I gripped his collar tighter as I closed my eyes and whispered the spell of Embla. With this spell I was granted temporary use of Evergreen's magic. I opened my now glowing eyes and tossed Fletcher into the pond. Using Evergreen's power I created a portal to somewhere dark and cold. "I'll make sure you NEVER come back to my home!" I say as I walk over to Fletcher. "Wait, I only wanted lotuses, I never wanted to hurt Evergreen, I just wanted to advance my powers." Fletcher said in a panicked voice "It's too late for that, the damage is done, you destroyed Evergreen for your selfish wants." I grabbed Fletcher's wand and broke

it in half. "Please don't do this," Fletcher begged but his pleas fell upon deaf ears. I dragged Fletcher to the portal and said my goodbyes as I pushed him in. When the portal closed I walked over to Olive. "Are you ok?" I said in a soft voice. I watched as my sister slowly got up looking slightly dizzy. "Yeah I'll be fine but what about the lotuses?" She asked it had completely slipped

my mind that Fletcher still had the lotus's when he went into the portal. "Oh no! Fletcher had all the lotuses!" I exclaimed "What do we do?" Olive asked but before we could answer a bunny hopped up into my arms then quickly hopped towards the pond. "Let's follow it, maybe it's trying to tell us something." Olive said as she began following the bunny. We followed the bunny back down the mountain that was now infected by the curse. "Are you sure we should follow this bunny?" I asked but before Olive could answer we were led to a small cave emitting light. "Should we enter?" Olive asked the bunny. The bunny brought us into the cave where we saw the source of the light. A shiny golden lotus encased in glass. I stepped towards the lotus and read the writing

out loud. "In great time of need heroes must step up to save the land they love. If you have found this lotus this means you are a hero, open the glass to bring back the beauty of Evergreen." As I opened the glass a large gust of wind hit our faces. "Do you think it worked?" I asked "Look for yourself!" Olive said. I turned around to find the familiar sight of bright green trees and clear waterfalls. I took in a deep breath and let the fresh forest air go through

The End

Made in the USA
Middletown, DE
18 August 2022

71480014R00020